BATS AROUND the CLOCK

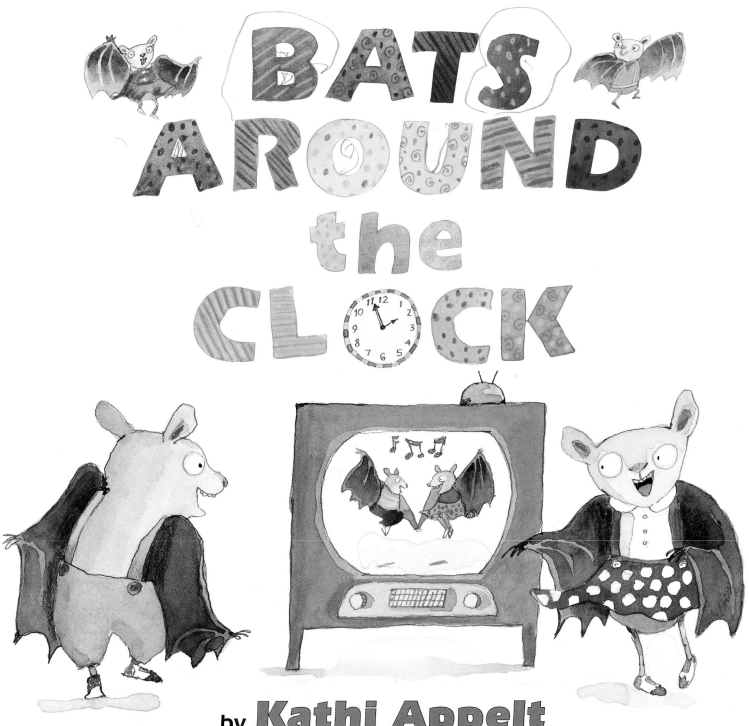

by **Kathi Appelt**

illustrated by **Melissa Sweet**

HarperCollinsPublishers

To rockin' rollin' Riley!
—K.A.

To Emily, who loves to dance
—M.S.

Bats around the Clock

Text copyright © 2000 by Kathi Appelt

Illustrations copyright © 2000 by Melissa Sweet

Printed in Singapore at Tien Wah Press.

http://www.harperchildrens.com

Library of Congress Cataloging-in-Publication Data

Appelt, Kathi.

Bats around the clock / by Kathi Appelt; illustrated by Melissa Sweet.

p. cm.

Summary: Click Dark hosts a special twelve-hour program of American Batstand,

where the bats rock and roll until the midnight hour ends.

ISBN 0-688-16469-2 (trade)—ISBN 0-688-16470-6 (library)

[1. Bats Fiction.   2. Rock music Fiction.   3. Stories in rhyme.]   PZ8.3.A554Baf 2000   [E]—dc21   99–15502   CIP

10 9 8 7 6 5 4 3 2 1

❖

First Edition

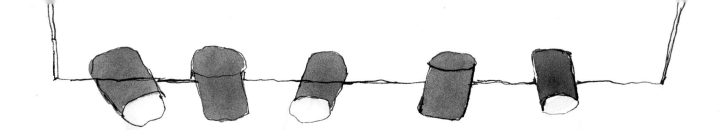

The cameras were rolling—
it was live from coast to coast,
a special twelve-hour program,
and Click Dark was the host.

At one o'clock Pacific time
those bats began the shrug.

At two o'clock Click Dark said, "Stop!
It's time to jitterbug!"

All across the nation,
all around the world,
on TV sets from here to there
those rockin' bats did roll.

With ponytails and bobby sox
at three they took a spin.

At four o'clock Click said, "Let's bop!"
and bats began the swim.

Sixty minutes later . . .
our host cried out, "Let's jive!"

With a swingin' and a swayin'
that's what they did at five!

There was rockin' in the rafters—
there was dancin' in the street.

Then they did the locomotion
and they boogied to the beat.

Well, they shimmied and they shammied
'til the clock turned round to six.
Chubby Checkers took the stage
and bats began to twist.

They twisted left and twisted right
until the hour of seven.
There was shakin', there was shoutin'—
it was rockin' rollin' heaven!

At eight o'clock the bats hip-hopped

and danced the hootchi-coo.

At nine o'clock those bats got down

and did the bugaloo.

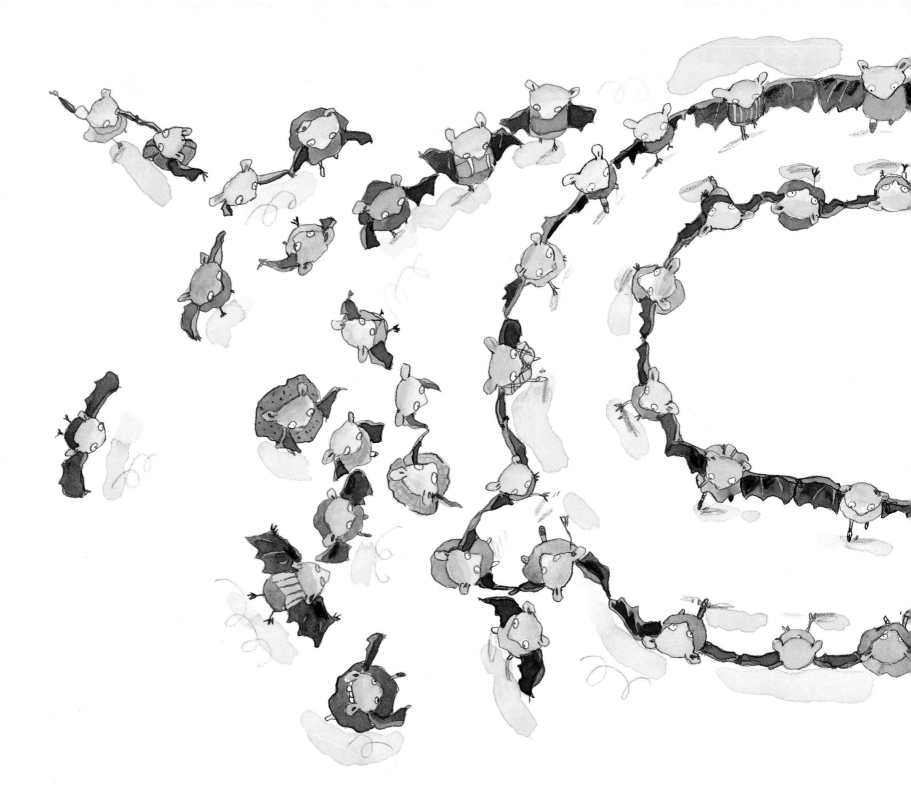

Just when it seemed they'd all poop out,
they broke into the pony,
and before the hour was over
they even did the hokeypokey.

The hokeypokey?

By ten P.M. those boogie bats

were groovin' in their boots.

At eleven it was plain to see
the group was cuttin' loose.

Now all across the continent
in dens around the nation
the audience was waiting
for the final demonstration.

The air was fairly crackling when
the moment came at last.

The clock struck twelve, and Click Dark yelled,
"Let's hear it for our guest!"

He leapt into the spotlight—
he belted out the blues.
The studio crowd went crazy
when they saw his blue suede shoes.

He was jumpin', he was jivin',
he was really in the groove.
He had those bats electrified
until his final move.

Then he sang to them so tenderly,
he sang to them so sweet,
when the midnight hour ended
the bats were off their feet.

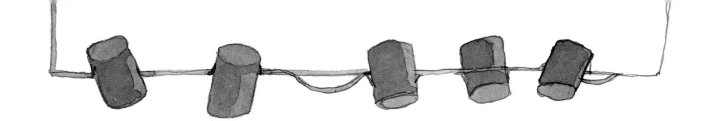

At last the show was over,
the studio was closed,
but tune us in again next year—
Click Dark will be the host.

In living rooms from north to south,
same time, same place, same station,
around the clock those bats will rock,
a twelve-hour bat sensation!